THE OLD WEST
& TIMES GONE BY

A Collection of Narrative Poems
About the American West

By Marshal T. Justice

copyright 2022 by Marshal T. Justice

Published by:

Jon H. Gutmacher, P.A.

Publishing Division

6391 Sagewood Way

Delray Beach, Fl. 33484

contact: gutlaw@gmail.com

Author: Marshal T. Justice
copyright 2022 by Marshal T. Justice
ISBN: 978-0-9984015-3-9

Published by:
Jon H. Gutmacher, P.A.
6391 Sagewood Way
Delray Beach, Fl. 33484
email: gutlaw@gmail.com

<u>Western Collection – Table of Contents</u>

Table of Contents i

List of Photographs iii

Introduction iv

The Shootist 1

The Cowgirl 8

A Tribute to Nat Love & Black Cowboys 12

Montana 14

Bass Reeves 29

The Story of Billy the Kid 31

Curtis Gray 33

Civil War 36

Lawman 38

The Hanging 40

The Drum Circle 42

Jessie & Wes 44

No Rain 47

Katie Elder - Ice Cold Katie 48

Calico Jack 52

The Ghost of Norma Jean 55

The Prayer Quilt 58

How the Marshal Died 60

Hatchet Joe 63

The Well 66

The Town 68

Howling Jack Riley 71

The Story of Stagecoach Mary 76

Exodusters – the poem 78

List of Photographs

Cover Photo: Nelli Bly, pioneer woman reporter, from the archives of New-York Historical Society/New York Public Library

Buckey O'Neill & posse (1889) ii

Custer's Command in North Dakota. iv

Annie Oakley and husband Frank Butler 7

Annie Oakley 11

Nat Love 12

Photos of African American cowboys on the range . 13

Unknown Western couple (1855) 28

Bass Reeves 30

Billy the Kid at a card game 32

Klondiker (1898) 35

Col. R.E. Rhodes, 5th Alabama Infantry 37

Wyatt Earp 39

Public Hanging (1897) 41

Chief Little Head, Crow Nation (1880) 43

Unknown female subject (cir.1880's) 51

Child with doll (1880). 57

Pioneer family in Nebraska (1886) 62

Seth Kinman, mountain man (1888). 65

Unknown frontier man and wife. 67

Paden Tolbert & posse (1892) 75

Stagecoach Mary. 77

Exoduster Poster (1878) 80

back cover: *Paden Tolbert & posse members (1892)*
                   (repeated photo)

back cover texture: courtesy of www.myfreetextures.com

Custer's Command in North Dakota

<u>Introduction</u>

You're about to read something truly unique. A book of original stories taking place in the American West that are really a series of narrative poems, more akin to the stories of Zayne Grey and Louis L'Amour than anything you'd think of as poetry. The book combines almost all of my newer works, as well as a few not quite as new. I'm a lover of the Western novels by Zayne Grey and Louis L'Amour, historical narratives on the Old West, and just about any movie or TV series on the old or new American West I can get my hands on. I've watched all four seasons of Yellowstone, all the Longmire series, grew up on Gene Autry, The Lone Ranger, Gunsmoke, The Rifleman, Have Gun Will Travel, and a whole lot more. I've seen every John Wayne movie three times over, same with Clint Eastwood, and every other western flick that's come my way. I've read a number of first person accounts from the Old West, subscribe to True West Magazine, have a library of books on the American West, and the list goes on. I just can't get enough.

You should know that my style of writing is unique. I write narrative poetry almost always consisting of complete original stories. In most of my work, my characters are ones I love and identify with, and a trait that runs through many of them in this book is "strong men, and even stronger women". Folks with honor, used to a hard, but rewarding life. In fact, I think you'll take an instant liking to most of them. To me, they come alive in the story, and many of these stories feature women, without whom the American West would never have been won, as well as three on African Americans who played a vital part in the development of the West, especially after the end of the Civil War.

Anyway, besides my love of the subject, where my stories come from, I couldn't tell you. Usually, I'll just be sitting around somewhere, or doing something unrelated – and an idea will hit me like a bucket of cement. Either I write it down then and there – or it's gone forever. It's ninety per cent inspiration, and ten per cent editing.

Last, I'd like to add one more word about the characters in my stories. They all take shape and come alive as I write them. Many seem like family, or old friends. Even though I realize they're fictional, I really feel for them, worry about them, and more than often shed a tear about their lives. In fact, there are some narratives I write that are so emotional to me, that I am unable to read them out aloud.

So, that's (so to speak) the story. These are all favorite stories of mine mostly set in the Old West, or no later than the early 1950's. Most of the characters I would be proud to call friend or family – and in a sense they are, and always will be. I hope you love them as much as I do.

<u>The Shootist</u>

John Robert Smith was no ordinary man
he wasn't born ordinary
didn't look ordinary
and sure as hell
didn't act it

Stood almost six foot seven inches tall
dark hair
cool blue eyes
thin, but muscular
with an easy laugh
his height, an anachronism in the late 1860's
and if you were a horse
you prayed
(assuming, of course, if horses could pray)
that John Robert picked some other horse than you
to ride

"John Robert"
as his friends often called him
(and there were many)
was a shootist
said to be the best in the far west
or at least, for sure, there were none better

He could shoot out the eye of a sparrow
with a Winchester
Take down a jack rabbit on the run with a Colt
and Damn, if he couldn't take out two birds
with one shot from that old two barrel shot gun
he sometimes brought out

And when the town got together for our annual
Thanksgiving Holiday
and Turkey Shoot
We had to give away a second prize - just to keep
everyone else interested
Cause John Robert always took first place
Not sometimes, but always

Now, of course
John's reputation spread
and there were always challenges
but when John would shoot a silver dollar clear thru the
center on a throw
That was enough for most of em

That was until that one fine spring day
when Sarah Jean Ketchem
first showed up

Sarah was something like a tornado
blowing thru the town
at a two hundred miles an hour

Nineteen years old
long flowing hair as red as the deepest sunset
A deep set of emerald green eyes that could burst a
young man's heart just from a stare
and a set of hips that could get a man in trouble
just for the lookin'

And sure as hell, don't stare too long
because she had the shiniest Colt revolver I ever saw
riding low on her right side

and it was there for business – serious business
and anyone with intelligence knew that
at just a glance

Sarah wasted no time when she first rode in
Walked into the Sheriff's Office and to the Sheriff's
face said:

"I'm Sarah Jean Ketchem.
"I'm nineteen years old
"I can rope a steer, brand cattle, and
"shoot faster and straighter
"than most men can ever hope to.
"I hear you have a shootist
"amongst you, and I will beat him, too!
"I want you to set up a meet, Sheriff!"

Well . . . that sure was an introduction!

That ol' Sheriff almost fell off his chair
at Sarah's words

But he'd been around a long time
and could tell right off that this gal was serious
and quite frankly – that Colt that rode low on her side
it sure had one hell of a convincing look to it
There was no doubt of that!

So the Sheriff just said:
"Young lady, it would be my pleasure to do so.
"John Robert needs a good match
"And I've got a fine feeling, you just might be it!"

Well, the contest started out smooth enough
John nodded to Sarah Jean to shoot first
and a can was set up on a fence at 50 yards
which Sarah promptly put into the air with a single shot
from the hip
straight and true
and then another, before that can hit the ground

Most of the town was there
and there was a whole lot of whistling and hooting
after that shot
in fact, even John nodded his head,
obviously impressed

But then, John Robert took his place and faster than the
eye could follow
Took that one can off the rail with his first shot
then sent it flying again - just like Sarah Jean
but faster
all before it hit the ground

"Damn!" I said out loud.
I didn't think anybody could do that!

But, there I was.
Saw it with my own eyes.
And, for sure, it was from the both of em!

Just mighty fine shooting
And to tell the truth - maybe just a little bit scary.

Of course, Doc Evers was the judge
And what Doc said – in this town – goes.

And Doc said it was a tie
and despite the speed of John's last shot
they still needed a tie breaker

A tie breaker?
How do you tie break that?

Well, old Doc pulled a new nickel from
out of his pocket
and showed it to both John and Sarah Jean
and then pointed to the sky

"I'm gonna throw it at the count of three
"You both get one shot
"John Robert, you go first."

Well, Ol' Doc threw that damn nickel so high
you could hardly see it
but before his arm was even down
you could hear the ping as John Robert's shot
hit it square

But then, another ping while it was still in the air

"Another ping?"
"Damn!"
It was Sarah Jean!

That young gal had drawn and shot before her turn!

Doc picked up that mangled nickel –
and held it up to the crowd
and everyone went wild

Men were dancing in the street, yelling
one woman fainted
little kids were running around in circles
one of the horses got loose – and to this day,
still has not been found
and John Robert and Sarah Jean Ketchum were both
rolling on the ground
laughing til the tears came out!

Oh, what a scene that was!

And everyone – yes everyone
sauntered over to the town's one saloon
and shared in a toast to John and Sarah Jean

Well, we tell that story often
but mostly at the town's annual
Thanksgiving celebration

And yes, John and Sarah did get married
and for sure – to each other

Had a family – two boys and a gal
and yes – they're all damn fine shooters, too
Just like their parents

In fact, they shoot so well
we had to add a third and fourth place prize
to the annual Turkey shoot.

Well, that's the story of John Robert and Sarah Jean
They lived a long time – had a good life

Grew old enough to see their children
have children of their own

All in the old west
in a place called
Montana

Well, did that story seem a bit far fetched? I admit I made up the entire thing, but low and behold, about four months after I wrote it I came upon the story of Frank Butler and Annie Oakley. Butler was one of the top sharpshooters of the late 1800's, and did exhibitions across the nation, as well as being a star in Buffalo Bill's Wild West Show. He met Annie Oakley in a shooting match in 1875 in which he had offered $100.00 to anyone who could beat him. Annie did – and the two were soon married, and lived together for over fifty years in a real love story. Maybe truth is stranger than fiction?

Annie Oakley & Frank Butler

The Cowgirl

Her hair was like a mass of tumble weeds
rolling across the open plains
it often got tangled into knots
said to surround her brain

A cowgirl to the bitter end
she could ride a horse thru the night
and shoot a Winchester straight and true
and "Damn!" . . . she could out drink
every cowpoke I knew!

I saw her while sitting in the local saloon
She took three shots of Tequila straight down
then grabbed a pool cue from the back
and shot a perfect round

I walked up slower than a damn slug
and started to say hello
but she turned around and headed out
with a cowpoke right in tow

"Damn!" I said under my breath!
I missed that gal again!
I wondered if I'd have another chance?
and I really wondered
when?

Well they say that karma's a Far Eastern thing
has little to do with the American West
but I couldn't put her out of my mind
although I did my best

And riding herd for the Circle B
I saw her coming near
she came on fast, riding right past me
and then she roped a steer

"Pardon me, Ma'am. Could you use some help?"
She looked up with some surprise
Shook off some dirt, tipped her Stetson hat back
Pushed some hair above her eyes

"Who the hell, you talking to?" She spat her words at
me.
"I can outride, out rope some ten of you!
"You better leave me be!"

"Damn!" . . . another chance shot to hell!
But at least I gave it a try
I turned my horse, but then looked back
and somehow caught her eye

"Hey, cowboy! I've seen you before!
"I know you've looked at me
"My name is Sam
"I ride this range
"my daddy owns the Circle B."

She laughed right then, and then turned back
she had to do a brand
and I pushed on
my head hung down
just another hired hand

But karma isn't all Far Eastern
it also exists in the American West
and when I hit the saloon a week later
somebody punched me right in my chest

"Hey, Cowboy! Never got your name!
"You know my name is Sam
"Do you shoot pool?
"I play for shots!
"Try to beat me, if you can!"

I almost fell over from that shot
my composure totally gone
and then I got my manhood back
ready to take her on

"My name is Wes. Sure, I'll take you on
"and beat you if I can
"I've seen you play
"You're quite a shot
"You might just be – the better man!"

She laughed at that
and grabbed a cue
and then began to play
she didn't miss
not once or twice
I finally had to say:

"I think I've had all I can take
"You're way too good for me!"
Then she grabbed my hand
pulled me out to dance

sorta like a jamboree

Well, we got on fast
maybe way too fast
but ever since that night
we're together when the stars do shine
and when the moon comes out at night

They promoted me to assistant foreman
but her daddy made it clear
if I didn't treat his daughter right
I'd have more than him to fear

Cause Sam can rope
and Sam can ride
and Sam can also fight
She's something like the untamed West
and I'd better
just treat her right

Annie Oakley 1902

I think most folks who read this book will not know that at least a third of American West cowboys were of African American descent, and were treated as equals on the trail and cattle drives. Black cowboys were famous, and were amongst the best out there. Men such as Nat Love, Bill Pickett, and Bose Ikard were well known, and sought after by the major cattle barons. Others became famous law men. But, where is any of this in the history books? When I started the research on this book I knew nothing of the rich past and contributions of black Americans to the American West, and felt cheated out of that knowledge once I found that out. I've written a couple of narrative poems about the more famous of them, and hope they open your eyes, as well.

<u>A Tribute to Nat Love & Black Cowboys</u>

Well, Howdy Mr. Nat Love
I see that you are black
but you can ride mighty awesome
plus, there is that gun you pack

You've fought lots of injuns
and rode the cattle drives
you've lived off the land for weeks and months
and yet - you have survived

A black cowboy back in the 1870's
back in the American West
There were plenty of you on the trail
some known amongst the best

On a cattle drive to Montana
or roping out some steers
the sky was your daily bunk house
you surely had no fears

Damn this lack of history!
So much I never knew!
This history about black cowboys
is most certainly – long overdue!

<u>MONTANA</u>

<u>CHAPTER ONE</u> – setting out

His name was Montana
he lived by a code
both parents were killed
just 15 years old

He buried them high
near a clump of tall trees
he cried for a moment
then fell to his knees

No kin folk
no friends
no one he could trust
he gathered his things
without too much fuss

He had just one horse
and a ragged old mule
but he headed out west
the wind blowing cool

His dad left a six gun
his mother a shawl
he had one set of clothing
and that was his all

And hopped in the saddle
and never looked back
he headed out quickly
lest the injuns attack

He'd heard that in Texas
a man could live free
so he headed out west
to find what would be

Then rode on for hours
til a town came in sight
he headed on in
somehow it felt right

The sheriff came out
and looked at the boy
dead tired, and so ragged
perhaps a might coy

But something felt special
perhaps it was fate?
and he said to Montana
"Son, you're riding quite late."

Montana got down
looked the man in the eye
wiped a hand caked with dirt
held it out – with a sigh

Said: "My name is Montana
"My parents are dead
"The Cheyenne took em from me."

That's all that he said

The sheriff knew the story
it was too often told
the injuns were raiding
the frontier was bold

And he said to that boy
a tear in his eye
"I could use some help here"
and that was no lie

Then he shook the boy's hand
and held it with strength
the bond there was instant
it had to be fate

And Montana agreed
he sure needed a place
he liked this man instantly
there was strength in his face

And the two walked together
to the town's only jail
with a room in the back
hung his coat on a nail

"You can stay here as long as you want
"as long as you work
"I've got lots of chores for you
"but there are also some perks

"I'll teach you to shoot
"I'll teach you to trail
"I'll learn you to read
"and tend to the jail

"And all of these things
"will make you a man
"it might take a few years
"but I'm sure that you can."

So, Montana agreed
and sat down on the bed
he was tired as dirt
and yawned as he said:

"I appreciate it, Sheriff
"I won't let you down
"I'll do what you say
"I'll stay in this town"

And the Sheriff gave a smile
and then closed the door
he felt Montana was ready
for what was in store

So, fell right asleep
with dreams in his head
remembering a hard past
a past that was now dead

And the Sheriff took a drink
in the town's one saloon
he wondered if he'd done right

he'd find that out soon

And was true to his word
taught the boy all he knew
forged a bond that was forever
. . . . like a father would do

<u>CHAPTER TWO – Trouble at the Saloon</u>

*The streets were all dusty
the sun came up burning the scorched earth
even though it was only dirt
it'd been two years since Montana rode in
and he wore a deputy's star on his vest . . . .*

"Hey there, Montana
"Sheriff's looking for you
"There's a fight at the saloon
"Sure, something to do!"

Montana grabbed a shotgun
and ran from the jail
stood sharp as cured iron
looked hard as a nail

The Sheriff was surrounded
it didn't look good
Montana hit one with the butt of the shotgun
his head split on the wood

"The next one gets buckshot!
"I'll blow you away!
"I can take two of you down!

"Now, who wants to play?"

The Sheriff shook his head
as the three men backed down
Montana did it again!
No one made a sound

He was now seventeen
Stood six foot or more
Two hundred pounds of pure muscle
With a heart that was pure

Eyes like blue diamonds
long blond and straight hair
walked kind of lanky
with hardly a care

Could shoot off the hip
was faster than fast
but always had a smile
a trait that would last

He idolized that Sheriff
would never let him down
and nobody messed with either
not in that town!

CHAPTER THREE – Shootout

The streets were all dusty
the town folk were too
a small church just for Sundays
that most of em knew

Cattle and ranches
were close to the town
the railroad came thru
to the west it was bound

He knew all the townsfolk
they knew him quite well
he'd grown lots of muscle
he could shoot straight as hell

And the sheriff and Montana
were almost like kin
proud of the boy
that he once took in

The saloon was the meeting place
it made lots of noise
gave the town a place to gather
town folk and cowboys

A single piano
that nobody played
long bar with a mirror
that somebody made

And a shot rang out suddenly
the Sheriff went down
a hole in his back
folks ducked to the ground

One ran for Montana
and told him the news
Montana ran out

gun ready to use

Then saw his friend bleeding
hardly alive
cradled his head
as the good Sheriff died

Then saw the man smirking
as he went for his gun
but Montana was faster
that killer was done

And he buried the Sheriff
high on a hill
all the townsfolk came out
it was a terrible kill

Not one man was dry-eyed
they all dressed in black
and Montana left that town . . . .
he never came back . . . .

CHAPTER FOUR – Back on the Trail

*When you lose a dear friend
who's closer than kin
it turns a man inward
makes other men sin . . . .*

Montana rode long
ten days and ten nights
found a town by a river
somehow got in a fight

Four men sought to beat him
but before they were done
Montana was winning
then drew out his gun

Nobody moved
one of em prayed
but the tallest of them
was really quite brave

"My name's Josiah Richards
"Let me buy you a beer
"You fought fair, and beat us
"You're a man I'd like near!"

It's strange how some friends
actually come to be
is it fate, luck, or random
maybe all three?

But Josiah and Montana
grew close right away
"two peas in a pod"
some later would say

And Josiah had a ranch
were cattle did roam
took half of the valley
a huge timber home

He offered a job
to his new fighting friend
and they were friends from that moment

yes, right to the end

CHAPTER FIVE – the Double Bar Ranch

Now Josiah had a sister
as pretty as could be
she could ride like the wind
her long hair flowed free

Lithe was her body
tanned was her skin
piercing green eyes
hair black as pure sin

And when she saw Montana
they both locked their eyes
he stumbled the introduction
he actually was shy

Rebecca laughed softly
she extended her hand
the electricity shot
Montana was instantly her man

And those two were soon married
the ranch rang with joy
and nine months later
she gave birth to a boy

And no place was happier
than the four on that place
black coffee every morning
smiles on each face

And Montana and Rebecca
walked hand in hand
the stars shown above them
it lit up the land

A steer bellowed in the distance
the moon rose so high
a cool breeze wafted over
as they sat under the sky

Then the days passed to years
the ranch did quite well
Montana was happy
no longer in hell

Then one night after supper
Josiah came back late
his face a bit ashen
all remembered that date

Josiah lit a cigar
handed one to his friend
"I'm sorry, Montana
"I'm afraid it's my end

"Doc says I've got cancer
"not much time to live
"I'll leave the ranch to you and Rebecca
"you've been my best friend."

Montana rose quickly
his cigar dropped to the ground
first his parents

then the Sheriff
not one left around

"No, Josiah!
"You can't leave us!
"You're more than a friend
"I'm not sure what I'll do
"if your life should now end."

And Josiah saw his friend weeping
so wrong for a man
put a hand on his shoulder
so he'd understand

"I don't want to leave you
"I'm happy, us three
"It was a blessing we met
"for Rebecca and me

Montana buried him carefully
on top of a hill
a stone with his name
carved with great skill

And the house turned all somber
no joy to be found
and Montana rode out
towards a rough frontier town

CHAPTER SIX – Gunfight

He was looking for trouble
he felt really down

he went right to the saloon
in the center of town

Had too much to drink
played a hard game of gin
saw the dealer sneak a card
and that did him in

"You're cheating, you bastard!
"I saw what you did!
"Put the money on back!
"If you want to live!"

And the dealer went for his gun
but he was too slow
Montana still quick
that's something you know

He shot that man deadly
between his two eyes
the man dropped like a rock
with a look of surprise

And nobody moved
then the Sheriff walked in
had the drop on Montana
but said through the din

"I'll be damned – it's Montana!
"I remember you, old son!
"I was a boy in the town
"From where you did come

"It was a fair fight, Montana
"I won't take you in
"what you did here was hard
"but it weren't no sin."

Then Montana left the town
back to his home
talked long with Rebecca
in a stark, somber tone

"I'm sorry, my Darlin'
"I did something bad
"I didn't realize til now
"All that I had."

And the stars shown above them
they lit up the sky
and they lived long and prospered
their love never died

CHAPTER SEVEN – All Things End

Now a man lives his life
through family and friends
each marks a spot
before his life ends

Monuments to his struggles
to his battles and loves
to his belief in one God
and the Heavens above

And the angels took Montana
at seventy three
his family buried him gently
under a tree

High on a hill
overlooking that place
where he first saw Rebecca . . . .
that gave his life grace

/ the end

*Archive photo - subjects
not known*

Bass Reeves isn't just another narrative poem. It's about a real person, the first black deputy U.S. Marshal west of the Mississippi. Bass was born a slave, but escaped into Indian Territory during the Civil War, and lived with the tribes. He later joined the U.S. army after the war, and was recruited as a deputy because of his familiarity with Indian Territory, and an uncanny ability to speak multiple tribal languages. He became one of the top lawmen of his time, and is credited with the arrest of over three thousand wanted men. His life story could take up volumes.

<u>Bass Reeves - one of the first black lawmen</u>

His name was Bass and it sure wasn't fish
Bass Reeves was black
and his gun was sure swift
he worked for Judge Parker
in the American West
was known far and wide
as one of the best

Bass was born as a slave in 1838
but there were better things for him
so much of it fate

Escaped to the Indian lands
while out on a trip
lived with the Creek
gave his master the slip

Served in the Union army
bought land and married his wife
had ten children with her but then
got bored with that life

Took a job as a U.S. Marshal
and earned quite a name
took in more than three thousand fugitives
each one grew his fame

Finally retired when Oklahoma became a state
took another job as a local lawman
but fell on bad fate

Caught a really bad disease
died in the year 1910
one of the finest black lawmen of the American West
did meet
his final end

Archive photo of
Bass Reeves

<u>The Story of Billy The Kid</u>

A hired gun just seventeen
he killed a man before
he came alone into the bar
just walked right thru the door

He wore a hat
it's brim quite wide
pulled down a bit too far
two six guns rode on either hip
as he walked to the bar

"You're awful young
"to be in here!"
The barkeep said to Bill
But the stare that followed
each those words
was a stare that coulda killed

"Just bring that bottle, and pour that drink!
"If you would like to live!
"My name is William Wright, old man.
"But they call me – Billy the Kid."

The barkeep stumbled behind the bar
as Billy said his name
he stuttered a quick apology
he knew of Billy's fame

"The drink's on the house
"I didn't know
"And if you want some more

"I'll put that bottle on the bar"

Just then the Sheriff walked through the door

"Billy the Kid!
"Your days are done!
"Put your hands on top your head!"

But Billy turned
Six guns ah blaze
And shot that Sheriff dead

That story's told around the bar
when things get really late
and the crowd grows hushed
as the story's told
about the Sheriff's fate

Now the posse's out
Billy's on the run
a reward is on his head
cause everyone in that frontier town

Just wants Billy
dead

Billy the Kid -- in high hat

<u>Curtis Gray</u>

Curtis Gray walked in the bar
he'd traveled very, very far
thru the mountains
thru the hills
after panning for gold
for years

He had one horse
he had one mule
and he was for certain
no one's fool
but it was long
since he took a drink
or saw another man

He plunked a coin right on the bar
they looked at him
from close and far
deciding what kind of man he be
this stranger from the hills

The barkeep asked him whence he came
and then he asked this stranger's name
and Curtis Gray looked him in the eyes
and froze him there . . .
like he had died

"I'm Curtis Gray – a mountain man
"I pan for gold throughout the land
"I'm tough as nails
"and twice as strong

"but I'm here – just for a drink"

And then a man rose from the back
he had a gun sticking from a sack
he approached real slow
and came abreast
and suddenly – punched Curtis
right in the chest

And Curtis looked at him - right in the eyes
and then he smiled
with great surprise
he'd thought him dead
these many years
and that ol' man almost
wiped some tears

"Oh, brother,
"How did you escape?
"those injuns had us
"at the lake
"I saw three of them
"take you down
"you should be dead, ol' son!"

And Blackjack Sam – that was his name
laughed at that – and life's great game
and pulled the scalps from deep the bag
that was below his gun

"Oh, Curtis – you old devil, you!
"I cannot die – I thought you knew
"I took em all

"I did em good
"and now they're dead
"as dirt!"

And then those two brothers
did embrace
both alive
through God and Faith
and drink they did
perhaps too much
and laughed into the night

For things were tough
back in those times
and in the high country
only grit
kept you alive
and some survived against the odds

But they were men
of steel

<u>Civil War</u>

On the battlefield they lay
not to see another day
limbs all shot
some torn away
it was too much for
mortal man

Their cries were heard from all around
their cries for help
no help was found
if this is war
then all men be damned
for it was far too much
to bear

"Please water, water!"
Their thirst so deep
as blood was lost
their thirst did peek
it tore my heart
it tore my soul
but there was nothing
I could do

And then one man could take no more
he stood up tall, canteen in store

and went upon the field of death
and gave them water
he did his best

And no one shot that man of faith
for he stood alone in God's Great Grace
and brought them water
far and wide
so some could live
while others died

I'll ne'er forget that bloody day
the lines of battle
now far away
how brave and true
t'was every man
in the War
Between the States

Col. R.E. Rhodes - 5ᵗʰ Alabama

This was the true story of Confederate Sergeant Richard Kirkland at the Battle at Marye's Heights in 1862. Kirkland was later killed at the Battle of Chickamauga.

<u>Lawman</u>

Lawman
six gun
by your side
badge on chest
horse to ride

You scour the badlands
far and wide
for those who kill
and steal

No place to run
no place to hide
you'll find them no matter
where they ride

Thru 'injun country
you thread real low
make sign of peace
where 'eer you go
you speak their talk
you make their sign
to survive this land
you respect their kind

You carry Colt
Winchester long
and when you aim
death sings his song
for your eye is steady
your hand is quick

few have your speed
to make it stick

And when they tire
you still move in
you never stop
'til they give in
and if they don't
they'll be dead by dawn
slung over their horse
to hell passed on

So tell me lawman
star on chest
of all your kind
who was the best?

Wyatt Earp

<u>The Hanging:</u>

Standing in the naked sun
all their lives to be undone
all for deeds to harsh to fathom
shaking there from head to bottom
in the naked sun

On the scaffold
six nooses hanging
breeze not blowing
clouds not moving
creaking pine planks
as they move up
standing in the naked sun

Crowd is sweating
preacher chanting
last words short
the end is coming
and the hoods slip on and over
as the rope surrounds each neck

All is hushed
yes, all is silent
all is over
but the waiting
and then the thud
as trap door opens
broken lives
all swinging free

They call it justice
the end to evil
a breeze sneaks in
that dusts the people
and creaks the ropes
of long dashed hopes
as hell awaits
those now dead folks

In the naked sun
In the naked sun

*Last public hanging in West Virginia
back in 1897.*

The Drum Circle

In the distance there was dancing to the
steady thump of the drums
drums that almost felt like your heart beating

A great fire roared and cracked in the
middle of the village
it's embers rising high into the sky
like the millions of stars above them
and I could see the warriors in their eagle head dress
as each mimicked the sound
and movements of the eagle
dancing and whirling their way around
the great circle surrounding the fire

"There was a time long ago when wolves ruled"
the medicine man intoned

He was old
Almost old as time itself, some had said
and He uttered his words in a low chant
each of us sitting close together
around a smaller fire
listening and watching while the embers from the fire
circled a lazy path into the evening sky

And as we listened
just as had our ancestors for hundreds of years
the story was told
passed on from one generation to the next
about the birth of the world

when the wolf ruled, and men
were but a dream in the sky

And I breathed in deeply while smoke rose
as the embers from the fire crackled and popped
sitting beneath a never ending sky
surrounded by the brothers of my tribe

Men who I hunted with every day
who I knew better than they knew themselves
as the millions of stars shown bright above us

While together we all joined in the chanting
the story of our People
as had all those before us
late, late,
into the night

Crow Chief Little Head
1880

Jessi and Wes

Jessi and Wes
were lovers from first sight
met in a bar
made love the first night

It wasn't that she was fast
truth being, Jessi was slow
but there was something between them
it just let her, let go

When they woke in the morning
they rode back to town
in Wes's old truck
then just drove around

Finally decided on breakfast
some bacon, some eggs
sat across in the diner
just two happy kids

And she laid down the law
if they were to be two
he had to be loyal
no cheating he'd do

And Wes shook his head in agreement
said he'd love her "til he died"
She put her head on his shoulder
and for a second she cried

Jessi and Wes were a couple
of that there was no doubt
they held hands when at home
held hands, when went out

And she held tight against him
and she kissed on the lips
and Wes always loved
his hands on her hips

Now of course they got married
had a family and a dog
hosted a family reunion
barbequed a big hog

With some fresh corn
and great cole slaw
and a whole mess of beans
sixty people or more
it was - quite a scene

But no one lives for ever
and neither did Wes
almost ninety years old
not feeling his best

And fell asleep one night
and never did wake
Jessi cried there for hours
for both of their sakes

Then took out a handgun
an old .38
made sure it was loaded
but it had to be fate

Just then her daughter arrived
stopped Jessi in time
she held tight to her mother
while both stood their crying

And Jessi did know
she'd miss him more than could be
but there was still much to live for
it's called family

Then Jessi moved in
with her daughter and kids
they had some great times
she was glad that she lived

But one night when the stars
shone really bright in the sky
she felt Wes's presence
and started to cry

Well, they buried her by Wes - under a tree
planted flowers that bloomed
that everyone could see

And grand kids and children
were there to say good bye
on a warm day in summer
under a crystal blue sky

This is a cowboy poem that takes place on a ranch out West where they've had a long and stubborn drought. It can be a hard life, and drought can take a man to the end of his soul. This poem is proof of it.

<u>No Rain</u>

It's been several weeks
without no rain
the 'crick is dry
life ain't the same

Another calf died
weak with thirst
I had to cry
my heart could burst

There's none but dust
around us here
we can hardly live
and that's in fear

Oh why, oh Lord
are things so poor
my crops all withered
there's nothing more

I've prayed each day
to have some rain
but at the end
it never came

And I'm about
to lose my land
and don't know what
to do

Katie Elder – Ice Cold Katie

She wasn't special to look at
But somehow, still seemed hot
worked at the only bank in town
it was her regular spot

And Katie was a strong woman
living all alone
in a house she built from scratch
a house that she made home

She went to church on Sundays
wore a proper dress
was kind to those around her
always tried to do her best

But when suitors tried to entice her
that, she firmly declined
except for the town Marshal
who she couldn't keep from eyeing

Well, they said Katie might wind up a spinster
if she didn't learn
to be nicer to the single men in town
or they might not return

But she and the Marshal
in the evenings
you'd often see them talk
and some days folks would notice
they'd just go for a walk

It was a sunny day in Kansas
the day was oh so hot
when five men rode into the town
guns drawn there on the spot

And two stayed back on horses
while the others ran straight in
they held up the bank that afternoon
an act of pure vile sin

Stuck a Colt out, right at Katie
thought she cower or probably faint
but Katie was ice
yes, cold as ice
and scared - that Katie ain't

She pushed off that varmint's barrel
while she grabbed for
her own gun
hidden under the counter
that robber soon was done

The other two bandits
turned, both in much surprise
Katie shot one from 30 feet
right between his eyes

He dropped like a lead potato
on the floor with a solid thud
Katie had the drop on the last one
as he turned quick to run

But Katie was much quicker
and Katie was really sharp
that next shot came so quickly
took that bandit
right through his beating heart

The other two bandits heard the fray
and knew they'd better run
they turned their horses straight around
disappeared in the noon day sun

Well, the town heard about Katie
and all what she had done
how she took on three damn bandits
and put the rest on the run

And the Marshal came on over
and then just scratched his head
he knew that Katie, for sure, was tough
But, just shot three men dead?

And while it might not have been proper
he proposed right on the spot
and Katie nodded her head in assent
their love was sure a lot

Well, the bank later threw a party
for Katie and Marshal Ben
and both were soon married
and had a lot of friends

And while Katie loved the Marshal
she had those steel grey eyes

always wore a Colt outside her dress
for sure, to none's surprise

And we called her "Ice Cold Katie"
as a badge, not something bad
she was a woman to be proud of
but, just
. . . don't make Katie . . .mad

Unknown female 1890's

<u>Calico Jack</u>

Calico Jack came thru the woods
some blood was on his vest
he held a Winchester in one hand
he'd just shot a man named Wes

Wes had it comin'
of that there was no doubt
he'd done some real bad things in life
caused Jack to take him out

He caught Wes in the woods one night
Wes was runnin' from the law
and Jack knew the woods
and knew the man
and was about to settle a score

He yelled at Wes to drop his gun
as he aimed on thru his scope
and then he fired a single shot
took Wes right thru
the throat

Wes fell down
to his knees
his hands clutched at his neck
he couldn't breath
he couldn't talk
his blood came spurting wet

And then he fell
straight on his face
for all the hell he'd done
and Jack came up
and kicked him once
and picked up Wes's gun

"You piece of dirt
"You piece of slime
"I hope you suffered long
"that little girl - that was my niece
"To Hell – I hope you've gone!

The Sheriff came and looked around
and shook his head, he knew
he put a hand on Calico Jack
then told him what to do:

"I'll say it was pure self defense
"As plain as the light of day
"and Jack, no man will question you
"but hear me, when I say:

"You shot him dead
"you had the drop
"it wasn't the cleanest kill
"but Wes was a snake
"the worst of kinds
"no one – will think you ill."

And with that speech and a deputy
they put Wes in a big ol' sack
then dragged him to a road quite near

and threw him in the back

Of a pick up truck with a Sheriff's star
there painted on the side
and dead damn Wes
went straight to Hell
as his body took that ride

For Justice is a straight up thing
that's been lost so much in time
but when Calico Jack
told his niece – what he'd done
she finally stopped her crying

It's been a good ten years
since that day
when Wes went straight to Hell
and Jack looked on with certain pride
as he heard the wedding bells

His niece grown up, and finally safe
in the arms of a loving man
and Jack stood proud with a smile on his face
Yes, he was quite the man

So, that's the story of Calico Jack
and the man he sent to Hell
and the fact that life goes on each day
I hope you're all doing well

The Ghost of Norma Jean

It was a story that my grandma told
about a crying sound
that happened in her house, so old
when there was no one else around

At first she heard it late at night
and then so ever brief
but every night at the stroke of twelve
it came with no relief

And grandma tried to find the source
And looked up high and low
And in the attic found a doll
that had an eerie glow

And all around were children's toys
each one was made of wood
made long ago
so long ago
but somehow still looked good

And the first doll looked so lonely
a deep sadness on its face
a child of wood in an ivory dress
with fringes made of lace

And grandma went to the town library
an old newspaper there ran her cold
it told the story of a little girl named Norma Jean
who had drowned at nine years old

They found her in the river
she'd fallen in and died
and all that town had loved her dear
and everyone had cried

And the house where she had then lived
was the one that grandma bought
found a photo of the child in that newspaper
saw what the river wrought

And then my grandma realized
who the crying each night was from
it was the little girl – now lost in time
her wandering never done

And grandma waited up that night
until she heard the cry
and then went up to the attic
saw a little girl
the child – the one who died

And called her name: "Oh, Norma Jean
"your parents love you so
"They're in the light
"Go find the light
"That is, where you must go!"

The child looked up
and understood
bright light streamed in the room
and everything felt good and blessed
it drove away the doom

And the little girl smiled at grandma
wiped wet tears right from her eyes
ran to the light
with sheer happiness
no need again to cry

And disappeared forever
with a smile on her face
and grandma said
she felt great love rush in
just like a deep embrace

We tell this story in hushed tones
and pray that all is well
for the little girl, named Norma Jean
there, buried on the hill

1880's child with doll

<u>The Prayer Quilt</u>

They say that angels are about
they say that prayers come true
they say that God won't let you down
no matter what you do

But My best friend was about to die
the cancer had her down
the doctors there just shook their heads
as each, they made their rounds

And so I began to make a quilt
each stitch made with a prayer
so God would somehow save my friend
If I could get it there

Each day her condition worsened
Each day my urgency grew
I had to finish the quilt before she passed
This was something that I knew

And each day I worked for hours
I never lost my faith
I knew the quilt would bring a cure
I'd work til really late

And somehow I finished just in time
placed the quilt across her chest
in a small bed close to family
where she planned her final rest

At first, she looked up slowly
Death hung dark about the room
but her eyes lit up when she saw the quilt
it pushed back all the doom

I placed it on across her
and watched her shed a tear
she held it close
it covered her
it wiped away the fear

Then the next day she felt better
and the next day even more
she was definitely getting stronger
she improved - her health in store

And one day she walked on her own
And still lives now, today
She's full of life, has lots of friends
but to me, she once did say:

"I don't know just what happened"
"When I felt the quilt I began to cry"
"The quilt felt like an angel's touch"
"I knew I would not die."

I thanked her then for saying that
her story left some tears
about the quilt
each stitch a prayer
long ago, so many years

How the Marshal Died

Found the marshal in his bed
shot him very very dead

Shot him first time thru the throat
watched him gurgle
life remote

Next shot caught him through the eye
that one surely made him die

Sadie Hanson was a rancher's wife
caused that rancher too much strife
she was something else to see
Never meant for marriage
just way too free

Snuck into the marshal's bed
the whole town knew
those gossips said
filtered back to her husband Sam
got his Colt
and made a plan

Next time he went for supplies
in truth he planned
a big surprise

Caught them both
that was his plan
shot her first
then shot her man

The sheriff was called
Sam gave no fight
he simply said
he made things right

"A man shouldn't worry about his wife"
The marshal paid . . .
with his life

They brought Sam before the judge that day
had a trial
right away

Twelve men sat in wooden chairs
listened to the evidence
like they really cared

Found him "Not Guilty"
"extenuating circumstances" said
Just too bad . . .
the marshal's dead

Sam went home
resumed his life
but never took . . .
another wife

Is there a moral to this story?
Think I should say?

Don't cheat with another
No, it's not
OK

For in the frontier
a man and his wife
are true to each other
and that there's
for life

1886 Pioneer family
in Nebraska

Hatchet Joe

Hatchet Joe was a mountain man
came into town one day
said he'd been in the hills
most of his life
but decided this town
he'd stay

No one could drink
the way he could
but I never saw him drunk
stood five foot ten
three hundred pounds
all muscle
quite a hunk

The sheriff made him a deputy
if trouble there would be
he'd call on Joe
his hatchet man
and the two of them would see

What the trouble was
in the town
usually a cowpoke drunk
but few men would face Hatchet Joe
like I said
he was quite a hunk

I remember when three men
took him on

it was a sight to see
the first one got a broken jaw
before Joe let him be

And then another
picked up a chair
tried to knock Joe around
but Joe grabbed the chair
and knocked him out
with a real hard thunking sound

The third man let out a yelp
swung hard at big Joe's head
but Joe was fast
yeah, really fast
nearly knocked that cowpoke dead

The stories of Joe
were mostly true
and he was a legend in town
but despite it all
regardless of his strength
he was one of the nicest men around

He wandered off
late in life
to lead a wagon train
and the stories never stopped coming in
about all his feats and fame

Well, they say he settled in California
and found a heap of gold

and died a rich man
with a wife and some kids
at almost ninety years old

Seth Kinman mountain man (1888)

<u>The Well</u>

The well was dug
bout twenty feet down
the water cool and clear
and if no rain did never come
the well was always near

My grandpa dug that
long ago
he lined it with hard stone
just him and grandma
on the frontier
livin' there alone

He said an angel told him where to dig
while he was deep in sleep
"Dig twenty feet down
"and line with stone
"The water will always keep."

The injuns then
were mighty bad
but their thirst just ran em dry
that well was magic to those heathen hearts
grandpa shared – so none would die

They drank their fill
they watered horse
and even traded skins
and grandpa smoked the pipe of peace
both whites and red men lived

As years they passed
the valley grew
other settlers found that place
and each man dug
that same length down
the water was God's grace

Now grandpa's passed
and grandma, too
and the injuns pushed away
but a town was born
called Weller's Place
that still stands there today

And the waters cool
and the waters clear
and the water ever flows
it's a place that's blessed
in a valley green
a place - everybody
knows

The Town

People would come from miles around
just to say
they'd been to town

The barber shop was always full
a razor shave
cost just one bill

The town saloon
served two kinds of beer
in mugs so tall
all times of year

And Saturdays
the town band played
in the square
the cowpokes made

The church bells rang
the preacher smiled
on Sundays folks
came there from miles

And never was a bad word said
cause the Sheriff was fast
as was his lead

It was a town
that had a school
one teacher there
was no one's fool

And the children learned
to read and write
that school marm taught
their lessons right

The shopkeeper ran
a general store
had most everything
and then some more
The town was sure
a place to be
families came in on Sundays
by twos and threes

They had a court
sheriff, marshal, and judge
justice was swift
that's just the way it was

Oh, I remember that town
yes, so clear
once the indians came
were met with fear

But, somehow the sheriff
knew their sign
and with his help
we all got along fine

We traded them
for real fine hides

no one was killed
on either side

And every year
a shindig made
in the big town square
a square dance played

We danced til midnight
we drank til dawn
it was a great time for everyone
we all got along

The town stayed prosperous
and slowly grew
the railroad came
and ran straight through

A telegraph line
keep all in touch
even had a place for town meetings
though it wasn't much

I'll remember that place
to my dying day
back in the Ol' West
long ago – from today

Howling Jack Riley

Howling Jack Riley came out on the plains
Indians there
all knew his name

They called him "Crazy Wolf"
They called him insane
And were afraid of his hatchet
that seemed to go for their brains

He was kidnaped by the Cheyenne
when he was just eight
they killed both his parents
but it musta been fate
cause they took him as hostage
like a dog in a cage
and made him do chores
as an eight year old slave

Well he soon knew their language
and somehow learned sign
he was quicker than all others
rode a horse like was flying

Shot an arrow so straight
was real mean with a knife
could throw another man down
in any ol' fight

And then he found a hatchet
when the Pawnee tried a raid
at eighteen years old
his life was remade

He was wild in that battle
his ax swung with death
he killed several Pawnee
and scared off the rest

Well, Crazy Wolf was a hero
soon a chief in that tribe
and great was his ability
to just stay alive

And he set off one day
when he saw the White Man
and was welcomed to a home
in Indian land

If not for his presence
those settler's would be dead
but the Cheyenne knew his story
and the word soon was spread
to let Crazy Wolf and his people
completely alone
those settler's were safe
safe in their home

Cause no one would battle
that crazy young man
who wore a feather on his head
in Indian land

Now, he learned the English language
better than most
learned to shoot a Hawken rifle
so good, his kin would boast

Took a stag down while running
almost a hundred yards out
let out a whoop when he did it
his friends all joined in the shout

Nobody had his prowess
no one had his skills
and once attacked by three Pawnee
he had another three Pawnee kills

His hatchet so red
with blood on his face
he scalped those three dead men
left their bodies in place

And his fame left the valley
and was known far and wide
by white men and injuns
who just wanted
to survive

Well, you're wondering how
Howling Jack
finally got his name?
Riley was the name of the settler's
who lived there on the plains

Who named him like a white man
and called his name "Jack"
and he loved those good people
and forever had their back

Saved em more times from danger
than anyone would know
and the injuns told stories
of when and where
he would go

And when the moon came out full
he'd howl at the sky
on top of a hill
he said he "never knew why"

But it made him feel whole
it gave him great peace
it was just something he had to do
his soul was released

That's the story of how
Howling Jack first got his name
but Crazy Wolf was more accurate
it followed his fame

And while he dressed like a white man
that feather sure told
this was a man of the frontier
now, just twenty and five
of his years old

And when Jack just turned thirty
he took an indian wife
went back to tribe
lived without strife
and one day disappeared
far into the hills
no one saw him again
most thought he was killed

But, I think that's just a story
I think he's still alive
he's out there in the hills
somehow managed to survive

And when the moon comes out in fullness
and the stars seem to shine
I can hear a faint howling
and I know that Jack's
. . . still . . .
doing fine

Paden Tolbert with posse

The Story of Stagecoach Mary

Her real name, Mary Fields
"Stagecoach Mary" was her fame
Don't matter which you call her
Both were her name

Stood six foot tall without shoes
two hundred pounds of pure strength
wore a six gun by her side
and weak - she sure ain't

Would cuss, damn, aloud
smoked a cigar
could throw a hard punch easy
often drank at the town's one bar

She delivered the mail in Montana
thru wolves, bandits, and snow
nothing would stop her
with a rifle and six gun in tow

Was the only woman in Cascade
allowed into a saloon
was loved there by all
worked right to her doom

They buried her there in Cascade
Biggest funeral ever had
the only African American who ever lived there
her death made all of them sad

For while she was a hard lady
she was still honorable and nice
she was respected by all the townsfolk
for all of her life

There was a short story
that I just have to tell
about a man that owed her money
that she didn't take too well

Was in the saloon drinking whisky
as the man sauntered by
She ran up and caught him
and let a hard punch fly

She knocked him out swiftly
and then was said to say:
"his bill is now settled"
Yeah – that was just Mary's way

Stagecoach Mary

<u>**Exodusters**</u> – the poem

Along the banks of the Mississippi
they came to be free
to find a home without violence
where they could just be

Far from former masters
and a South full of hate
it was time to strike out West
before t'was too late

The Klan would often hang em
or subdue them real good
they were poorer than dirt
and dirt did no good

It was time to find freedom
where they could live free
as hard working equals
that's where they must be

Came Benjamin Singleton
Henry Adams as well
both had a plan for their People
to lead them from Hell

Formed a series of committees
to move from the South
hired steamers on the Mississippi
where freedom was their shout

Many headed to Kansas
where black men could be free
The Homestead Act promised land
and land there would be

Over forty thousand made the journey
to the American West
and founded black towns all over
and hoped for the best

They called themselves "Exodusters"
like the bible did say
like the Jews who left Egypt
a "Promised Land" far away

And to Kansas
Colorado
Missouri, and more
they came by the thousands
a new life – was in store

There were families
There were children
Both husband and wife
Strong stuff they were made of
for their coming new life

And they built there their homes
with God as their guide
and with prayer and hard work
they all managed to survive

They took part in the story
of the American West
and helped it to grow and get strong
they passed – every test

That's the story of the Exodus
I doubt that you knew
they were cowboys
they were businessmen
and many famous, too

They came out to settle
in a land that was free
and slavery just a bad dream
of what once did be

Ho for Kansas!

Brethren, Friends, & Fellow Citizens:
I feel thankful to inform you that the

REAL ESTATE

AND

Homestead Association,

Will Leave Here the

15th of April, 1878,

In pursuit of Homes in the Southwestern
Lands of America, at Transportation
Rates, cheaper than ever
was known before.

For full information inquire of

Benj. Singleton, better known as old Pap,

NO. 5 NORTH FRONT STREET.

Beware of Speculators and Adventurers, as it is a dangerous thing
to fall in their hands.

Nashville, Tenn., March 18, 1878.